KT-429-475

■ この絵本の楽しみかた

● 日本文と英文のいずれでも物語を楽しめます。

● 英文は和文に基づいて詩のように書かれています。巻末 Notes を参考にして素晴らしい英詩文を楽しんでください。

● この「日本昔ばなし」の絵はかっての人気絵本「講談社の絵本」全203巻の中から厳選されたものです。

■ About this book

● The story is bilingual, written in both English and Japanese.

● The English is not a direct translation of the Japanese, but rather a retelling of the same story in verse form. Enjoy the English on its own, using the helpful Notes at the back.

● The illustrations are selected from volume 203 of the *Kodansha n* ... *Pi* ... *ries.

Distributed in the United States by Kodansha America, Inc., 575 Lexington Avenue, New York, N.Y. 10022, and in the United Kingdom and continental Europe by Kodansha Europe Ltd., Tavern Quay, Rope Street, London SE16 7TX.
Published by Kodansha International Ltd., 17-14 Otowa 1-chome, Bunkyo-ku, Tokyo 112-8652, and Kodansha America. Inc.

Copyright © 1993 by Kodansha International Ltd.
All rights reserved. Printed in Japan.
First edition 1996.
Small-format edition 1996, 2000.
03 04 05   10 9 8 7

LCC 93-18500
ISBN 4-7700-2100-3

www.thejapanpage.com

日本昔ばなし

うらしまたろう

URASHIMA AND THE KINGDOM BENEATH THE SEA

え●かさまつ しろう

Illustrations by **Shiro Kasamatsu**
Retold by **Ralph F. McCarthy**

KODANSHA INTERNATIONAL
Tokyo · New York · London

They tell me that once,
   far away, long ago,
A fisherman named
   Urashima Taró,
Who lived with his parents
   somewhere near the sea,
Had quite an adventure—
   I think you'll agree.

とおい　むかしの　おはなしです。
うらしまたろうは　おとうさんと
おかあさんと　うみべの　むらに
すんで　いました。

Taró loved to fish by the seashore and dream.
He'd angle for mackerel, flounder, or bream
And dream of the Dragon King's palace of gold
He'd heard of in stories the fishermen told.

6

たろうは　うみの　そこに
あると　いう,
りゅうぐうじょうへ
いく　ゆめを　みるのが
すきでした。

One day, walking home
    on a path through the trees,
Taró met some children
    who'd gathered to tease
A little sea turtle.
    "Don't hurt him," he said.
"I'll give you a coin
    if you free him instead."

ある　ひの　ことです。
たろうは　こどもたちに
いじめられて　いる　かめを
たすけて　あげました。

8

Taró took the sea turtle down to the sea.
"It's dangerous here. Go back home, now," said he.
The turtle swam off, looking back now and then,
As if to say "Thank you. I'll see you again."

かめは　たろうを　なんかいも　ふりかえりながら
うみの　そこに　きえて　いきました。

いえに かえった たろうは,
かめを たすけた はなしを
りょうしんに して,
その やさしい こころを
ほめられました。

Taró told his parents
        the story that night.
"You'll never go wrong, son,
        by doing what's right,"
Said Father, and Mother said:
        "Isn't that true?
Taró, we're so glad
        we've a good boy like you."

One day a year later,
    Taró was out fishing
And wishing and dreaming
    and dreaming and wishing
When, to his surprise,
    as he sat there afloat,
A giant sea turtle
    swam up to his boat.

"Hello there, old friend Urashima Taró!
Remember me? You saved my life once, you know.
Now I'd like to do *you* a favor, you see.
Come down to the Dragon King's palace with me!"

つきひは ながれました。
その ひも うみに でて つりを して いると,
たすけた かめが あらわれて
「うらしまたろうさん, わたしは あなたに
　たすけられた かめです。
　きょうは その おれいに
　りゅうぐうじょうに ごあんないいたします。」
と, たろうを さそいます。

He didn't think twice—well, why should he? Would *you*,
If *your* greatest dream was about to come true?
He sat on the back of his sea turtle guide,
Prepared for the world's most incredible ride.

たろうを　のせた　かめは,
うみの　そこふかく
もぐって　いきます。

かいそうや
さんごの
あいだを
くぐりぬけて，
りゅうぐうじょうへ
むかいます。

18

Deep down dove the turtle,
   then down deeper still,
To curtains of seaweed
   that covered a hill,
Then on through the curtains,
   to what lay below—
A forest of coral
   that waved to and fro.

たろうは めの まえに あらわれた
りゅうぐうじょうの うつくしさに おどろかされました。
おしろが きんと エメラルドで できて いるのです。

Then on through the forest, and lo and behold:
The Dragon King's palace, all emerald and gold!
And there at the gate, seven beautiful maids
Awaited Taró with their hair up in braids.

The seven maids led him, and seventy more
Walked softly behind down a long corridor,
Up to a great building, the grandest of all
In all of the palace—the Dragon King's Hall.
And there stood a vision before young Taró—
The Dragon King's daughter, fair Princess Otó.

たろうは　さかなたちに　あんないされて,
りっぱな　ごてんに　はいりました。
そこには　おとひめさまが
たろうを　まって　いました。

Amazed at her beauty, Taró bowed his head.
She smiled at him gently and tenderly said:
"I thank you for saving the sea turtle's life.
His sister-in-law is my third cousin's wife."

なんと　うつくしい　おとひめさまでしょう。
「かめを　たすけて　いただき,
　ありがとう　ございました。
　どうぞ　ゆっくりと　おすごしください。」
おとひめさまは　たろうに　おれいを　いいました。

A banquet was held for the guest from the shore,
With seven maids dancing, and seventy more
All gathered around to make music and sing
And serve food and drink that was fit for a king.

その　ひは　たろうの　かんげいかいが　ひらかれました。
おいしい　ごちそうと　おさけが　ふるまわれました。

おとひめさまも　おんがくに
あわせて　おどりました。
たろうは　あまりの
うつくしさに
こえも　でないほどでした。

And late in the evening, fair Princess Otó
Arose to dance all by herself for Taró
And sing him a song as she tiptoed and twirled:

"You're welcome to stay here in our little world.
Down here there's no sorrow, no anger, no fear,
No reason to leave—all you've dreamed of is here."

29

You can't really
   blame him for
      wanting to stay.
He lingered for
   many a long,
      lazy day,
And soon he lost
   all sense of time,
      it appears—
The days became weeks,
   and then months,
      and then years.

たろうは　くる　ひも
　くる　ひも　たのしく
すごして　いる　うちに,
つきひの　たつのも
わすれて　しまいました。

But one night our hero sat dozing, and dreamed
Of Mother and Father. How lonely they seemed!
They scanned the horizon for signs of Taró,
Who'd left to go fishing some three years ago.

ある　ひ，　たろうは
かえりを　まちわびて　いる，
さびしげな　かおを　した
りょうしんの　ゆめを　みました。

The next day Taró told the princess, his love,
He had to go back to the land up above.
"It grieves me to think of my parents alone.
I'll miss you, but I have a home of my own."

たろうは　いえに　かえる　けっしんを　して、
その　ことを　おとひめさまに　うちあけました。

いよいよ　わかれの　ときが
きました。
おとひめさまは　たまてばこを
たろうに　わたすと,
こう　いいました。
「はこを　けっして
　あけては　いけません。」

"So be it," she said with a tear in her eye,
And gave him a gift to remember her by—
A box decorated with ivory and gold.
"Don't lose it," she said, "and you'll never grow old.
Return with it someday to make me your bride.
But don't ever open it—*don't look inside*!"

The turtle was summoned to carry Taró
Back home to the land he'd left three years ago,
And as they departed, escorted by fish,
The princess cried: "Come back as soon as you wish!"

たろうは　りゅうぐうじょうを　あとに　しました。
おとひめさまは　なみだを　ながして　みおくりました。

The sea turtle left Taró off at the shore,
Then called out "Farewell!" and dove under once more.
"I'm home!" cried Taró, running up to the land
And straight to the spot where his house used to stand.

かめは　はまべに　たろうを　つれて　かえりました。
「さようなら。　たまてばこは
けっして　あけては　いけませんよ。」
と　いって,
かめは　うみの　そこに　きえて　いきました。

Imagine his shock—the house wasn't there!
There wasn't a trace of the place anywhere!
And as he walked on, he kept thinking: "How strange!
I can't believe even the pine trees would change!"

はまべに　たった　たろうは　おどろきました。
じぶんの　いえの　かげも　かたちも　ありません。
そこには　ただ，くさが　はえて　いる　だけです。

たろうは　とおりかかった
おじいさんに　たずねました。
「うらしまたろうの
　おとうさんと　おかあさんを
　しりませんか？」
「うらしまたろう。
　はて，だれの　ことだろう。
　はいはい，おもいだしました。
　たろうさんは　うみへ　つりに　いった　まま，
　かえって　こなかったんです。
　でも，その　おはなしは　3びゃくねんも　むかしの　ことですよ。」

At last, around sunset,
  he met an old man.
He stopped him and said:
  "Tell me where, if you can,
The parents of young
  Urashima Taró
Have moved to—
  their house is gone!
    Where did they go?"

"What's that? Urashima?" the man said and smiled.
"That name's from a legend I heard as a child—
A boy who rode off on a turtle one day
Some three hundred years ago, some people say."

What? Three hundred years ago! How could that be?
It didn't make sense—he'd been gone only *three*.

45

At last he remembered
  the box in his hand.
"That's it!" he thought,
  setting it down on the sand.
He untied the ribbon and lifted the lid . . .
And that was the last thing Taró ever did.

　　　　　　　　かなしみに　くれた　たろうは
はこを　あければ　すくわれるかも　しれないと　おもいました。
そして，　ふたを　あけました。　なかから　しろい　けむりが
たちのぼり，　かおに　かかりました。　すると　どうでしょう。
かみの　けは　たちまち　しろく　なり，　うらしまたろうは
３びゃくさいの　おじいさんに　なって　しまいました。

He'd thought
  the box might
    hold some clue
      to the truth—
But out
  flew all three
    hundred years
      of his youth!
His hair
  turned snow-white,
    and he felt
      stiff and cold.
That's right—
  young Taró
    was three hundred
      years old.

Notes うらしまたろう ♦Urashima and the Kingdom beneath the Sea♦

p.4　quite an adventure たいへんな冒険　you'll agree あなたもそうだと言うでしょう

p.6　mackerel サバ　flounder ヒラメ　bream タイ　the Dragon King's palace of gold 竜王の黄金の宮殿

p.8　tease いじめる　Don't hurt him いじめるな　instead そのかわりに

p.11　now and then ときどき　as if to say ~ ~と言うかのように

p.13　You'll never go wrong 道をふみはずすことはない　by doing what's right 正しいことをすることで　a good boy like you お前のような良い子

p.14　to his surprise 驚いたことに　as he sat there afloat 船にゆられて腰を下ろしていると　do you a favor 今度はあなたに恩返しをする

p.17　think twice ためらう　why should he? なぜ彼がためらうでしょうか　Would you あなたはためらいますか　if your greatest dream was about to come true? あなたの一番の夢が今にも実現しそうなときに　prepared for ~ ~にそなえて

p.19　Deep down dove the turtle カメは深くもぐった　seaweed 海草　on through the curtains 海草のカーテンをいくえもこえて　to and fro あちこちへと

p.21　awaited ~ ~を待っていた　with their hair up in braids 髪をあみあげて

p.23　corridor 廊下　there stood a vision before young Taró 太郎のまえに夢のような姿が立った fair Princess Otó 美しい乙姫

p.25　Amazed at her beauty 彼女の美しさにぼうぜんとして　bowed ~ ~を下げた

p.27　banquet うたげ　fit for a king 王にふさわしい

p.29　arose to dance all by herself 立ってひとりだけで踊った　as she tiptoed and twirled つま先だってまわりながら　sorrow 嘆き　no reason to leave 帰る理由はありません　all you've dreamed of is here あなたが夢見たものは全部ここにあります

p.31　blame him for wanting to stay 太郎がとどまりたかったのを責める　lingered for many a long, lazy day 何日も何日も長いのんびりとした一日をすごした

p.32　sat dozing うたた寝をしていた　scanned the horizon for signs of Taró 太郎の姿が見えないかと水平線を見やっていた

p.34　It grieves me to ~ ~することは私には悲しい

p.37　So be it そうなさいませ　with a tear in her eye 目に涙をためて　gift to remember her by 乙姫をおもい出すよすがの贈りもの　decorated with ivory and gold 象牙(ぞうげ)と金で飾られた　to make me your bride 私をあなたの花嫁にするために

p.39　was summoned to ~ ~するように呼ばれた　escorted by ~ ~につきそわれて

p.42　There wasn't a trace of the place anywhere! どこにも跡形もなかった
I can't believe even the pine trees would change! 松の木までかわるとは信じられない

p.44　is gone なくなった　from a legend I heard as a child 子供のころ聞いた伝説の

p.45　How could that be? どうしてそんなことがありえるのだろうか　It didn't make sense わけがわからなかった　he'd been gone only three 3年いなかっただけだ

p.46　That's it! これだ　untied ほどいた

p.47　hold some clue to the truth ほんとうのことの手がかりが入っている　out flew all three hundred years of his youth 太郎の若さの三百年がすべて消え去った
（佐藤公俊）

●和英併記●日本昔ばなし　うらしまたろう

かさまつ　しろう／ラルフ F. マッカーシー

発行日　1996年9月27日　第1刷発行
　　　　2003年7月4日　第7刷発行

発行者　畑野文夫

発行所　講談社インターナショナル株式会社
　　　　〒112-8652　東京都文京区音羽1-17-14
　　　　〔電話〕03(3944)6493
　　　　ホームページ www.kodansha-intl.co.jp

協力　講談社児童局

印刷　大日本印刷株式会社　　製本　黒柳製本株式会社

落丁本、乱丁本は購入書店名を明記のうえ、講談社インターナショナル業務部宛にお送りください。送料小社負担にてお取替えいたします。本書の無断複写(コピー)は著作権法上での例外を除き、禁じられています。

© Kodansha International 1996 Printed in Japan
ISBN 4-7700-2100-3